Girl TALK

PET HOTEL

Any creature that leaps, runs, flies or swims is welcome at Tangletrees Pet Hotel...

Have you read all the

PET HOTEL

books?

Welcome to Pet Hotel

Twice the Trouble

The Non-Stop Runaway

Pet Hotel Detectives

More
Pet Hotel animal stories
out soon!

1

WELCOME TO Pet Hotel

Mandy Archer

BBC

First published in 1998 by BBC Worldwide Ltd
Woodlands, 80 Wood Lane, London W12 0TT

ISBN 0 563 38094 2

Printed and bound by Mackays of Chatham plc

Contents

1

A Strange New House

As far as Becky Ashford could see, her little sister, Sophie, was totally unbelievable. She had sobbed for hours when she'd discovered she had to leave Maryford Primary in South London. But now Sophie seemed to have completely forgotten she was supposed to be upset. Becky watched in amazement, as she ran around their new place at 5, April Close like a lunatic, opening up cupboards and screeching with delight every time she found a new hiding place.

"Come on, Becks, cheer up," begged Sophie, as she hared round the empty rooms, "there's so much to *explore*!"

Sophie always made the best of things — the way she saw it now, moving to Sussex did offer lots of advantages for both of them. The new house in the country was nearly three times the size of the old flat, and there'd be no more rows because they'd each have their own bedrooms. But the best thing about the move was that the family were escaping the fumes and pollution of London, something which really upset their dad's asthma.

The journey down in the removal lorry had been hilarious. Sophie and their dad, Dan, had been singing daft songs at the tops of their voices and waving like the Queen at the cars they passed. But neither of them had been able to persuade Becky to join in. She was trying so hard to be brave for her dad's sake, but saying goodbye to her friends at school had been terrible. Her best friend Simone had promised to write, but she knew it wouldn't be the same. Most of all, she missed her mum dreadfully. The girls' parents had got divorced six months ago and Sarah Ashford now lived in a vineyard in France. Although she phoned lots, poor Becky was taking things a bit hard. With every passing mile she could feel a horrible ache growing inside her. She sunk lower and lower into her seat, cuddling Albert, her sad face turned to the window so the others wouldn't notice her tears.

Albert was the girls' beloved white West Highland Terrier. Their mum and dad had bought him for them when they were still together and so Becky was sure he understood how she felt. He was three years old, with a cheeky little face that he'd always tip to one side when anyone spoke to him. It was just as if he was really listening.

When they drove past the sign for Haresfield village, Dan and Sophie cheered at the top of their voices. Becky took a deep breath — maybe they were right about moving to Sussex. Haresfield *did* look like the sweetest place she had ever seen, full of pretty cottages and quiet, tidy lanes. And Dan had chosen the house very carefully. He'd even made sure that they were near Clayton, a large local town, so that if the girls ever got bored, they would still be able to do all the things they had enjoyed in London.

Lying in bed that night in her brand new room, even Sophie had to admit she felt a bit odd. Albert had been allowed to sleep on the end of her bed as it was the first night, but Sophie still felt as if she was having a lonely sleepover in somebody else's bedroom.

Sophie's eyes quickly looked round the room for her dressing gown and spotted its cord sticking out of a box full of her magazines and comics. She slipped out of bed and tiptoed towards the box, tripping over her tape player on the way. Trying to be as quiet as a mouse, she then crept out of the room, leaving Albert curled up in a sleepy bundle on her duvet.

"Hello Sophs," murmured Becky, when Sophie slipped into her bed and snuggled up next to her,

"I was hoping you might come in."

Becky had been trying to get to sleep for ages. After spending what seemed like hours tossing and turning, she'd started reading her book of ballet stories with a torch under the covers. Normally, after a chapter or two, she'd drop off quite easily, but tonight she didn't even feel drowsy.

"Can I stay in here with you, Becky?" whispered Sophie.

"'Course you can! But be quiet in case Dad hears, OK?"

"All right, I'll try. This funny new house has made me think about Mum, that's all," she said.

"I know how you feel, but I'm sure she'll come and see us soon," Becky replied. "Now come on, close your eyes and at least *try* to get to sleep. Things always seem better in the morning."

Sophie kicked and fidgeted a bit until she got comfy, then closed her eyes tightly. Becky did the same, wincing as she pulled her long dark plait out from under her little sister's elbow. She was glad Sophie felt better. She only wished *she* could cheer up, too...

"Good afternoon, you two! Come to join me at last?" laughed Dan when his sleepy daughters shuffled into the kitchen the next day.

A bleary-eyed Becky sat down at the table. "What's for brekkie, Dad?"

"Forget breakfast, Rebecca, I'm nearly ready for lunch!" her dad teased as he handed over the cornflakes. "I was expecting you up hours ago, especially as I've made a special effort to serve the full works — bacon, eggs, tomatoes..."

Dan's grand offering was cut short by the ear-splitting chorus of the doorbell and the smoke alarm ringing at the same time.

In a sudden burst of teamwork, Dan leapt on a chair to tackle the alarm, while Sophie ran to the hall and Becky rescued the scorched black slices of toast with a fork.

"Someone for you, Dad!" Sophie bellowed over the noise.

Dan had now managed to wedge a broomstick underneath the alarm to shut off the terrible din. With one hand still holding it, he turned to his daughter. "For me?" he said, confused. Then he remembered. "Yes of course! Would you ask Mrs Fitzgerald to come through to the kitchen, love? I've sort of got my hands full."

Becky stared blankly at Dan as Sophie went back to their guest. Who was this Mrs Fitzgerald? Her mind raced — surely her dad couldn't have found a new girlfriend already?

"Mrs Fitzgerald said she's just, er, wiping the mud off her wellies," Sophie whispered, carefully pulling the door behind her. "Who is she, Dad?"

Becky chuckled. Her cheeky sister always got to the point.

"That, Miss Nosy, is someone in Haresfield that you're going to get to know really well," Dan answered with a smile. "What's more, I can absolutely guarantee that you'll like her."

Becky was over like a shot. "But I thought you didn't know anyone in the village yet?"

Before Dan could say another word, the stranger burst into the room, her face beaming. "Hello, dears!" the old lady exclaimed, "*wonderful* to see you safe and sound in Haresfield!"

"Hi, Angela! How are you?" smiled Dan. He moved to get up, then checked himself as he realised that the alarm would be set off if he moved an inch. "Sorry, we're in a bit of a muddle. Here are Sophie and Becky."

Mrs Fitzgerald put down her bag and moved forward to shake hands. "Good morning! I'm so pleased to meet you both."

The girls grinned. There was something about

Mrs Fitzgerald that made it hard *not* to smile. A large, bustling lady with rosy cheeks, she was dressed in a floral skirt that clashed with her sweater and padded jacket. Her hat had feathers pointing out in all directions, some of which had been bent as she'd rushed through the kitchen door in her large, green wellington boots.

Sophie couldn't bite her tongue any longer. "Dad, how do you know Mrs Fitzgerald?" she asked in a loud voice.

"Haven't you told them about me yet, Dan?" the lady cried. She turned to Sophie and nudged her in the ribs. "I bet you're wondering who on earth I am!"

Sophie went red and nodded.

"When I came down with Gran to see the new house, we found an agency that put us in touch with Angela." Dan explained. "She's going to be your childminder when I'm at work. As soon as I met her I knew that she'd be perfect for you girls."

Sophie and Becky exchanged surprised looks. In London, their Auntie Kath had always been there after school.

"Well, we can't leave you on your own, can we?" Mrs Fitzgerald laughed. "Someone's got to make sure you don't oversleep! When the new term starts next Monday and your dad has to go back to work, I'll come round, make breakfast and take you to school everyday."

"Mrs Fitzgerald lives in an enormous house in the village called Tangletrees, which you'll love. In the afternoons, you'll go there until I get back from London," their dad added.

"Now, please don't be nervous about anything, we're going to have a great time!" their new childminder promised, her eyes twinkling.

"But... what will we *do* there?" Sophie asked bluntly.

"Well, Billy will keep you amused for a start," said Mrs Fitzgerald.

"Billy?"

"Yes. He's the Shetland pony that lives in the meadow at the back of Tangletrees."

"Wow!" exclaimed Sophie, clapping her hands and jumping onto her dad's knee. Even Becky couldn't help feeling excited — a real pony to visit!

"I don't want either of you to worry about next Monday. I wouldn't leave you with anybody I didn't trust," Dan told them. As he spoke, he stretched out an arm to cuddle Becky, too, forgetting he was still holding the broomstick. The stick crashed down, missing little Albert by a centimetre. The dog yelped in fright and skidded towards Mrs Fitzgerald's wellies, as the alarm began deafening everyone in the kitchen again. In an instant the old lady had swept the Westie up in her arms and begun calming him down. Bertie licked her face in reply.

"That's Albert," shouted Becky above the din. "I think he likes you!"

"He's simply brilliant!" Mrs Fitzgerald yelled back.

"I'm sorry it's a bit of a madhouse here today Angela," apologised Dan, clambering on the chair again to shut off the alarm once and for all.

"Please don't mention it," she smiled and placed Bertie carefully in Becky's arms. "Now shall I hold the broomstick while you fix the alarm? Then we can all settle down to a fresh round of toast and a good chat!"

Sophie and Becky both giggled — it looked like their childminder was going to fit in pretty well!

2

Lost!

"I'm sorry, girls, but it looks like the trip to the cinema is off," said Dan, as he banged the boiler tank with frustration.

"But it was our treat before starting school tomorrow!" wailed Sophie.

"That was before the central heating broke down. You'll soon be complaining if I don't get it fixed, and I'm going to be too busy to mend it when I get back to work."

Becky frowned miserably. She'd been really

looking forward to seeing the new Disney film. She'd also thought that it would take her mind off the fact the holidays were nearly over. They'd spent most of the first week in April Close playing on their bikes, or climbing trees in the fields at the back of their house. Starting St Sebastian's tomorrow was going to be a big shock to the system.

"Dad, *please*, it's only September. It won't get really cold for ages!" she moaned.

"I'm sorry, Becky, but it needs sorting out. We'll go next weekend, I promise." There was nothing Dan hated more than plumbing jobs, and he knew he would need the afternoon to make sense of the house's baffling heating system.

"Well, if we're not going to Clayton, can we take Albert out for a walk instead?" Sophie asked, her dark eyes twinkling.

"'Course you can. But be back by five so we can get your uniforms ready for the morning."

"I'll make sure, Dad," promised Becky, although her words were completely drowned out by Albert's barks of delight. You only had to mention the word 'walk' and the little dog burst into a frenzy of excitement. He trotted off happily to the hook where his lead was hanging, peeking over his shoulder to make sure that the girls were following him.

"If you don't sit still for one second, Bertie, we won't be going anywhere," smiled Becky as she tried to fasten the lead to the Westie's bright red collar. Albert just licked her face in reply.

Before shouting their goodbyes, Sophie fetched his ball and a few doggie treats. Upstairs, she could hear their dad tapping the boiler tank with his spanner. He'd be busy for hours.

It was only a few minutes stroll from their home to the wide open fields and countryside at the base of the Sussex Downs. Once clear from the windy lanes of Haresfield, Becky let Albert run off the lead. He immediately tore away, a white streak racing round the girls in great circles.

"Come on, Bertie, see if you can break the record!" bellowed Sophie, as she sent the blue ball flying into the air.

The ball game was an ongoing competition between the three of them. Each of the sisters took turns in hurling the ball as far as possible, then Albert ran like the wind to pick it up. No matter how far they threw it, the Westie would always chase the toy, although sometimes it took him a while to bring it back when he got over-excited. Once, last summer, they'd got into big trouble when Sophie had thrown the ball into a pond by mistake. Bertie had disappeared into the water within seconds, leaving the girls to wade in after him. It was Becky that eventually caught the dog and carried him out. Although he was covered in thick black mud and pondweed, Albert had still been proudly clutching the ball in his mouth.

The game went on for ages, until Becky looked down at her watch. "Come on you two, it's half-four. We'd better head back."

Sophie and Albert bounded over, skidding to a

halt in front of the older girl. "OK. I don't think I can run another step anyway!" Sophie giggled.

Becky slipped the Westie's lead back on as they set off towards home. As they wandered along, the girls chatted nervously about the new school year at St Sebastian's, Sophie throwing and catching the ball above her head.

Suddenly she misjudged her throw and sent the blue rubber ball whizzing way off in front of them. It looped overhead, sailing straight into someone's back garden.

"Oops! Sorry, I wasn't concentrating," she said with a shrug.

"Oh no! Look at Bertie!" cried Becky as the little dog ducked back through his lead and bounded off towards the ball. The thick hedge behind the house didn't even stop him. He squeezed himself through the greenery in search of his lost toy.

"Look what you've done now!" cried Becky, the lead hanging loosely in her hands.

"*You* were meant to be holding him, not me," Sophie replied crossly.

They began calling through the bushes, but the Westie was nowhere to be seen. Becky searched in vain for a back gate to sneak through. "It's no good, if he's playing with his ball he'll have forgotten all about us."

"Well, I'm going to fetch him! Dad'll go mad, otherwise."

"No way! You can't climb through someone's hedge like that. We'll just have to wait," Becky decided. "He should come back if we keep calling."

Her sister began pushing and scraping her way through the privet anyway. "I'm not waiting here all day," were Sophie's closing words, as she finally forced her way through. "We'll be back in two minutes, Becks."

Seconds slowly dragged themselves into minutes as Becky peered uneasily into the hedge. She softly called out Sophie's name, her mind racing.

When five o'clock came and went, Becky realised something was wrong. She had no choice

but to follow her adventurous sister. Although the thick bushes were dark and uninviting Becky got through in the end, with a few cuts and scratches.

"He — hello?"

She was faced with a small, empty garden. Becky started hunting by the climbing frame and shed, but it only took her a moment to see no one was around. Finally she summoned all her courage and banged on the back door. She'd just have to explain what had happened to whoever lived here.

No one answered.

After two more agonising minutes, Becky gave up. Her heart was pounding like a drum. Where were they? Now it was serious, she knew she had to tell her dad.

Becky burst through the hedge and set off on the run of her life back to April Close. Tears were streaming down her face as she bolted over the fields and through the village streets. She had tried so hard to be responsible — how was she going to tell her dad that she had managed to lose both Albert *and* her little sister?

3

The First Day For Everyone

Becky took a deep breath and wiped her tear-stained face as she waited at the front door in April Close.

"Back at last!" grinned Sophie, as she opened the door.

Becky stared at her little sister in disbelief. Looking past Sophie, she spotted Albert curled up lazily at the top of the stairs.

"Come in and meet Isabel, she goes to St Sebastian's too!"

A small blonde girl of about Sophie's age came

into view. “Your dog got into my garden,” she explained with a friendly smile.

Becky felt a wave of relief, followed by a surge of anger. “How could you leave me out there on my own?” she cried. “I was so worried about you both!”

“I’m sorry, Becky. When I climbed through and met Isabel I must have got carried away. She asked me in to meet her cat, Barnaby. He’s the best cat ever! He’s going to be the father of kittens in a few weeks and…”

“The mother cat belongs to the old village vet, Donald Hall,” added Isabel helpfully.

“Wait a minute! What do you mean you got ‘carried away’?” Becky’s eyes fixed angrily on her sister.

“Well, it was all so interesting I forgot about the time. It was nearly five so I thought that you would have gone back to get ready for school tomorrow,” Sophie tried to soothe her big sister. “So Isabel’s dad gave me and Bertie a lift home. He’s upstairs now helping Dad fix the central heating.”

Becky knew Sophie hadn't meant to upset her, but she was furious. She could feel even her fingers tingling with anger. "You are *so* thoughtless! I was waiting ages for you! You said you'd be back in a couple of minutes — how could you, Sophie?"

Sophie looked down at the floor.

The red-faced girl pushed past the two seven-year-olds and stomped upstairs to her room. On the landing, she swept past her dad and caught a glimpse of Isabel's father before she slammed her door with a deafening thump.

Becky dived face down on her bed, sobbing. All she could think was that none of this would have happened if they were still living in London.

"Well, how was it?" Sophie asked her sister as they joined the crowd of pupils streaming out of St Sebastian's at home-time the next day.

She and Becky had made up the night before. When Sophie realised how thoughtless she'd been (and received a strong telling off from her dad), she had apologised at once to her big sister.

Becky could never stay cross with Sophie for long, anyway. She just wished that her sister would take time to think before wading into the thick of things.

The girls reached the end of the school drive. "It wasn't as bad as I thought it was going to be, Sophs," Becky confessed. Everything had been a bit confusing at first — finding classrooms, canteens, the assembly hall, remembering names — but most people seemed friendly, and her class teacher, Mrs James, was really nice.

"Mine was OK, too. I'm in Isabel's teaching group — ace or what?" Sophie laughed. "Now, where's Mrs Fitz?"

"Watch it, cheeky — you can't call her that. We don't even know her properly, yet!" said Becky with a grin.

The girls linked arms as they looked out for their childminder. Mrs Fitzgerald had arrived bright and early that morning, so organised that no one would have believed it was her first day.

Dad had left for the station shortly after her arrival, but only after asking the girls a hundred times if they were going to be all right. It felt a bit odd kissing him goodbye in the new house, but Mrs Fitzgerald wouldn't allow tears. She soon cheered them up by cooking a fantastic pile of pancakes as a special treat. Sophie thought it was the best breakfast she'd ever eaten! Afterwards, she had taken the girls to St Sebastian's, promising to look after Albert while they were at school.

"Yoo-hoo! Becky and Sophie Ashford! Over here, please!"

Mrs Fitzgerald was waiting for the girls in her large green Land Rover, her face beaming from corner to corner. "Come along. Hop in, that's it!"

Albert went crazy with delight when the girls clambered in next to him on the front seats. Becky and Sophie made loads of fuss of the Westie, and he licked their faces back to say hello.

"Now, before we set off for Tangletrees, I'd like you to meet Charlie. He's just behind you."

The girls buckled up and turned round to see. In the back, Mrs Fitzgerald's elderly golden retriever was stretched out contentedly. As he caught their eyes, Charlie's tail began banging on the floor, wagging energetically even though the rest of him stayed perfectly still. "I think his games with Albert have worn him out! We did have some fun in the back garden this afternoon, I can tell you," she chuckled. "You were right about that blue ball being his favourite, Becky!"

Before she should say any more, Mrs Fitzgerald had to swing the steering wheel round to avoid hitting a post. She wasn't very good at talking and driving at the same time.

Within a few minutes, their first bumpy journey to Tangletrees was nearing an end. Mrs Fitzgerald swung the car round past Haresfield village church and screeched to a halt in front of an imposing old house, standing all by itself in the lane.

"Welcome to Tangletrees, young ladies — I hope you'll like it here," said Mrs Fitzgerald, waving her hand in a grand gesture. "Come and meet my housemates!"

As they went up the drive, Becky realised Mrs Fitzgerald's rambling home was enormous. The central red brick building seemed to have all manner of extensions, turrets and attic rooms protruding from it, with a different pair of brightly-coloured curtains shining from every window.

"You've got a goat as well as a pony? Brill!" squealed Sophie as she spotted an old, white billygoat tethered on the back lawn.

"That's Oscar, he cuts the grass for me. Come on in, there's more inside!" she said, as she poked around in her pockets for the front door key.

Tangletrees proved to be a Noah's Ark full of pets, and the sisters were duly taken round to meet each and every one. As well as Oscar and Charlie, they were introduced to a pair of identical ginger cats (each called 'Puss') and a host of visiting pigeons lodging in Mrs Fitzgerald's coop. Finally, their childminder whisked herself off to make tea, leaving Sophie and Becky playing in the back meadow with Billy.

"Can I give him another carrot, Becks?" whispered Sophie, as they stood quietly stroking his beautiful chestnut mane. As she spoke, she scratched the pony's ears, giggling as he closed his eyes and gently nuzzled at her arm.

"Hey, it's my turn!" said Becky, although she handed the carrot over anyway. "Dad really made a good choice with Mrs Fitzgerald — she's amazing!"

As Becky spoke, they both saw the large outline of their childminder picking her way towards them through the back garden. She was carrying a sloshing bucket of water for the pony.

"Time to wash your hands, girls, tea's almost ready."

Mrs Fitzgerald beamed with pleasure when she saw Billy's contented face with its lovely white stripe down the centre.

"Gosh! You've really made a new friend there, girls. Let's give him his water and then pop in for a bite, eh?"

"OK, Mrs Fitzgerald!" said Sophie.

"Great! Oh, and do feel free to call me Mrs Fitz — most people do round here," she grinned.

Becky may have imagined it, but she was sure the old lady had winked at her when she'd said that.

4

The Haresfield Vets

By the time Dan arrived at Tangletrees to take the girls home, Sophie and Becky were settled in the snug kitchen, playing with the ginger cats. A young man was sitting in the oak rocking chair in the corner, chatting at a rate of knots. It was Jake Green, the young vet from Haresfield surgery. He had popped round to drop off a winter blanket for Billy, which he had been promising to lend Mrs Fitzgerald for ages.

Jake was great fun. With his thick, auburn

hair, battered jeans and silly jokes it was hard to believe that he was such a well-qualified expert on animals. He had been a vet for two years now, and had a special interest in unusual pets like spiders and exotic birds.

Mrs Fitzgerald introduced Dan, while Jake continued to tell all the Haresfield gossip. Becky wasn't sure how much of it was true, but his version of events was so funny it kept her glued to her seat.

"Have you met my colleague, Donald Hall, yet?" Jake asked his audience. "Now, he's a real local character."

"No, but I made friends with Isabel Wilde yesterday. Her cat, Barnaby, is going to be the father when his Rosie has kittens," Sophie answered. As everyone seemed so interested, she couldn't help spurting out what else she'd heard. "Actually, Isabel also told me that Mr Hall is very fierce — a real old grouch in fact!"

"Sophie!" exclaimed Dan, embarrassed.

Becky pinched her sister hard to warn her to

shut up, but Jake just laughed.

"Ah, so you've heard the rumours too, have you?" he said in a serious voice. "I think this Isabel might be right. I certainly wouldn't mess with old Donald Hall if I were you. He's the grumpiest man in the village!" Jake spoke in a deep voice, opening his eyes really wide for maximum effect.

"Rubbish! I've been friends with Donald for years and we've always got on famously," said Mrs Fitzgerald.

"Ah, but you've never got on the wrong side of the man, Mrs Fitz. He can be an ogre!" Jake continued, getting completely carried away with his story.

Mrs Fitzgerald just tutted and told Jake to stop being silly.

"Well, I've got a bit of gossip myself," said Dan mysteriously to his daughters. "Mum called today to say she's coming over to see you both for Christmas."

"Brilliant!" cried Becky, while Sophie jumped

out of her chair in excitement. They hadn't seen their mum Sarah since the start of the summer holidays.

"I knew you'd be pleased," smiled Dan. "She's going to write soon and let us know what flight she's on."

As he spoke, their dad swallowed hard to stifle a yawn. "Now, I think after my hectic day at the office, I'd better take you girls home before I drop off!" he chuckled. "Thanks for having them, Angela." Dan lent over to shake hands with the young vet. "Great meeting you, Jake!"

"Look forward to seeing you soon, Dan," said Jake, smiling.

"I'll see you tomorrow morning," announced Mrs Fitzgerald, her eyes twinkling affectionately at the girls. "Don't oversleep! And make sure your dad has an early night, Becky, that train ride to the city is very tiring."

Becky nodded, but before they could go, Sophie insisted on taking their father round to say goodnight to all of Mrs Fitz's pets.

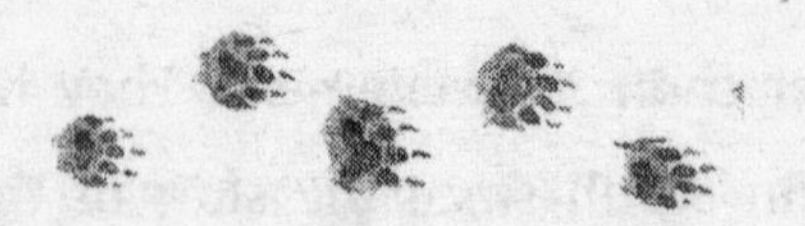

With a house like Tangletrees to visit every afternoon, it didn't take Becky and Sophie very long to really feel a part of Haresfield village. In just a few weeks, Sophie felt like she had been at St Sebastian's for years. Becky started to settle in too, although her favourite part of the day was after school at Mrs Fitz's, helping out with the pets.

Mrs Fitzgerald allowed the girls to feed the animals, putting Becky in special charge of grooming Billy. Whenever she came out of the back door at Tangletrees with the red grooming tray in her hand, the pony would walk across the meadow so he was standing ready at the fence by the time she got there. While Becky rubbed down his chestnut back and legs with a strong brush, the mischievous Shetland would lean his head round to softly nibble her coat. She was certain he was enjoying the grooming just as much as she was!

Albert seemed fascinated by Billy. When Becky

was with him, the little dog would weave in and out of her feet, sniffing the pony's hooves. Billy didn't seem to mind, although Becky was always worried that the terrier would get squashed by mistake.

While Becky was busy with the pony, Sophie usually played outside with the dogs or went out on her bike with Isabel. One Thursday afternoon, Isabel and Sophie were haring through the village at top speed, taking it in turns to trail each other, their legs lost in a spinning blur.

"Right, the last one to the top of the hill is a moron!" screamed Isabel.

Sophie's bike wasn't as new as Isabel's, but she was just as good at racing and began pedalling like mad. The blonde-haired girl was way in front, but Sophie was gaining as they stood up in their seats to tackle the steep climb up Haresfield Hill.

"You'll never make it, Sophs!" Isabel cried, hair streaming behind her.

"Wanna bet?" Sophie pedalled extra hard. Somehow she managed to sail past Isabel and cross the brow of the hill in front.

"I did it!" she shouted, lifting the front of her bike up in a wheelie and turning round to Isabel in triumph.

"Watch out! What are you *doing*?!"

Sophie turned back in horror to see she was about to hit a tall, spindly man who was crossing the road. Somehow, she swerved out of the way in the nick of time. Sophie's brakes squeaked noisily as she ground to an emergency stop.

"I'm really sorry, I was..."

"I know exactly what you were doing young lady. You were riding like a lunatic!" snapped the old man, waving his arms about angrily. "Now be careful in future or I'll tell the police!"

With that, the thin gentleman pulled his cap over his eyes and stomped away, muttering as he went.

Isabel drew up her bike next to Sophie's as they watched his retreat in stunned silence. "We've really done it now, Sophie," she said, worriedly. "That's Mr Hall! I hope he doesn't tell my dad about our bike races — he would, you know."

Sophie couldn't believe it. "I didn't even get the chance to say sorry properly." Jake was obviously right about Donald Hall.

"Well, I'm definitely avoiding him in future," decided Isabel, "even if his cat is going to have Barnaby's kittens."

Sophie agreed. She was itching to see Rosie's kittens when they were born, but she didn't want to risk running into *him* again.

5

Looking After Dan

School had finished, and the girls were doing their afternoon rounds at Tangletrees, making sure the pets had been fed and settled for the evening. They had now reached the back garden to visit Oscar the goat. Becky had mixed up his feed earlier and was holding the bucket out for him, while Sophie was raking the floor of the shed that was Oscar's makeshift stable, so it would be clean and comfy for the night. Although it was quite small, it had everything the goat needed — a soft straw floor, a water trough and a door with its top half cut out so that Oscar could look around.

The sisters were locked in serious conversation.

"I think we should say something to Mrs Fitz," said Sophie with a frown. She could see their childminder waving at them from the kitchen window as she spoke.

Both girls waved back.

"No, we can't," said Becky. "Dad wouldn't like it. You'd better keep your voice down too." She smiled as Oscar began gobbling down his meal, but her eyes showed how anxious she felt inside.

"Well it can't just go on like this! I'm really worried about him," exclaimed her little sister. "Dad is worn out!"

"He fell asleep in front of the TV again last night," muttered Becky.

During the last few weeks Dan Ashford had been looking more and more exhausted. He had bags under his eyes from the long hours and could barely stay awake later than the girls. What was worse, he never had any time to do anything for himself, especially as he had to take his accountancy work home with him most weekends.

"Well I think it's up to us to do something about it," said Sophie.

Becky raised her eyes to heaven. "OK, but what can any of us do?" she argued.

Sophie put down the rake and dug her hands into her green puffa jacket. "Shall I write a letter to Mum?"

"Don't you dare!" snapped her sister. "Mum might think he can't cope!"

"Well, have *you* got any bright ideas?" said Sophie, sulkily.

Becky would have answered, but she was diverted by the nudges of Oscar. The billygoat had got through the last of his food and had started gently butting the bucket for more. She stroked the goat's head, showing him the empty pail so he could see it was all gone. "There's no more tonight, Oscar!" she whispered.

"He can come in the shed now, Becky, I've

finished," announced Sophie.

The girls led the animal in and carried on with their discussion. Becky sat on the corner of the water trough, taking in the sweet smell of the freshly-raked straw. "I think Auntie Kath knows how he feels," she confided. "I heard him on the phone to her last night, after you went to bed."

Sophie looked up in surprise. "You never said she phoned!"

"I wanted to tell you when we were on our own," Becky explained. "Anyway, I heard Dad mention that he's very tired."

"Oh, poor Dad!"

"He also said that he's getting quite lonely," continued Becky. "Because he's always in London, Dad hasn't had much time to make any friends around here."

"But he really likes Jake," said Sophie, puzzled.

"Yes I know. But he only gets a chance to see Jake if he happens to be round when Dad comes to pick us up from Tangletrees." Becky undid the goat's lead collar and gestured for Sophie to come out of the shed. As she pulled the door closed, Albert trotted out from behind the goat's legs. The Westie had been happily following them round for ages.

"I just don't know what we can do," Sophie moaned in frustration. She hated not being able to help.

"We'll think of something," Becky answered. "I'm going to groom Billy now, you'd better go in and learn your spellings for that test tomorrow."

Sophie put on a sulky face, but she knew she'd be in trouble if she didn't do it. "All right, I'll take Bertie, then. He only gets in the way otherwise!" said Sophie. Albert barked for some attention and so she bent down and scooped the little white dog up in her arms.

Becky nodded and ran over to collect the pony's grooming kit. Sophie made her way to the house to warm up in the kitchen with Mrs Fitzgerald.

"Any chance of a choc-chip cookie, Mrs Fitz?" bellowed the brown-haired girl as she approached the back door.

"Of course! Come and join us," came the reply.

Sophie turned the doorhandle.

Us?

Donald Hall was sitting in the rocking chair, staring straight back at her. Even through her surprise, Sophie thought the old man's face looked just as fierce as the last time they met.

"It's YOU!" they both said at once.

Mrs Fitzgerald stood up in surprise. "Do you two know each other, then?"

Donald nodded irritably. "This, Angela, is the thoughtless little rascal who nearly knocked me over in the street!"

Sophie turned scarlet and swallowed hard.

"Well, I know Sophie would never do something like that on purpose!" said Mrs Fitzgerald, soothingly. "She and her sister Becky really are quite wonderful children."

"I'm very sorry, Mr Hall," Sophie forced herself to speak.

"Yes, you should be!" Mr Hall scratched his head, and paused thoughtfully. "Well, all right then. But just you watch it in future!"

Mrs Fitzgerald smiled and reached for the cookie jar. "Peace offerings all round," she said as she passed the container to Sophie.

After a couple of biscuits, and several cups of tea from Mrs Fitz, the smart old vet seemed to soften up a little. Soon, he began telling Sophie about his work with animals. She nearly forgot how terrified she had been to come face to face with him again. His stories were certainly far too interesting to abandon for the sake of learning her spellings.

Mr Hall explained that he had founded Haresfield surgery in the 1950s, and that he'd probably looked after every kind of animal over the years. Now he worked part time, sharing the responsibilities with Jake Green.

He also described his cat, Rosie, who was expecting kittens at Christmas. Although this was exciting news, the old man seemed worried because he had planned to spend a month with his daughter in Australia at that time. It was clear that Mr Hall really loved his cat, and was concerned about leaving her.

"If you like, you can come round to visit Jake and me at the surgery, find out more about what we do," the old vet suggested, in between slurps of hot tea.

Turned towards the stove, Mrs Fitzgerald smiled broadly to herself. Donald Hall's bark was worse than his bite, but even she was surprised at how much the stern old man had melted this afternoon.

"Excellent!" burst out Sophie. "I mean, yes please!"

"Good, good," Mr Hall nodded. "Well, come on Saturday, then! And bring the family won't you. I'd like to meet your father."

The vet looked over to Mrs Fitzgerald as he spoke. Before Sophie had come in, the old friends had been having a serious chat about the Ashford family. Mrs Fitzgerald was just as worried about Dan as the girls were. She could see how worn out the poor man was getting. To try to help, she had started cooking a hearty meal for him each night — but most evenings he was too tired to eat much, anyway.

But luckily, Mr Hall's visit this afternoon had given her an idea that could solve everything...

6

A Visit To The Vets

"Quick, they're here!" squealed Sophie. She was sitting on the landing windowsill, peeping through the net curtains. Sophie had spotted the patchwork hat that was Mrs Fitzgerald's favourite, bobbing along up the path to 5, April Close. Her retriever, Charlie, was trotting alongside her, tugging eagerly at the lead.

"I just need two minutes and I'll be ready!" promised Dan, who was running late as usual. "Pop down and answer the door."

"Hurry up, Dad, *please*," moaned Becky. Today was the day of their visit to Haresfield surgery and neither sister wanted to be late.

Sophie leapt down the stairs two at a time to open the front door.

"Morning, Mrs Fitz!" she cried, giving her childminder a hug hello.

"Hello, dear!" Mrs Fitzgerald answered. "All ready to go?"

"Nearly." Sophie bent down to stroke Charlie, who was wagging his tail like a mad thing. "Becky's just trying to get Dad organised."

Mrs Fitzgerald chuckled to herself as Sophie raced upstairs to hurry them along.

Within a few moments, Becky and Dan were in the hall, grabbing coats and scarves as Albert circled wildly around them.

"Right! I'm finally ready, Angela," said Dan, beaming. "Shall we set off for the surgery?"

"YES!" roared Becky as she hooked up Bertie's lead. It was only a ten minute walk to Haresfield, but Sophie decided to ride her bike alongside the group. She took extra care to cycle sensibly this time. With Mr Hall looking out for them, she certainly didn't want to run over anyone else!

Haresfield veterinary surgery was actually a row of three tiny cottages that sat in the High Street on the edge of the village green. When Donald Hall had founded the practice, he'd knocked through the dividing walls that separated the homes.

"Welcome, welcome," smiled Mr Hall as he greeted his guests at the front door. "You can leave your bike out the back, Sophie. No more racing I hope," he added with a wink.

"Morning, Donald," smiled Mrs Fitzgerald, removing her hat. "Meet my friend, Dan Ashford."

The two men shook hands vigorously. "Delighted, I'm sure," nodded the old vet. "Now come and have a look round. It's a bit shabby in places, but interesting nonetheless." He led them into the large reception room, which was filling up with people and animals. Amongst the casualties was a tiny green budgie in a cage and an enormous Old English Sheepdog with a bandage tied round one of its front legs.

After sniffing the air hastily, Charlie and Albert both started barking and raising the hackles on their backs. They were looking at a lady with a cardboard box who was sitting quietly in the corner.

"Now come on you two, calm down," warned Mrs Fitzgerald firmly, although the pair took no notice. "Donald, the dogs will have to wait outside. I think there could be a cat in that box that's getting them a bit over-excited!"

The owner stroked the box protectively and nodded.

"Good idea." Donald led the two dogs out into a sideroom, passing them into the care of the surgery receptionist, Mrs Williams.

After a few more 'hellos', the tour began. As well as the reception and treatment rooms, Donald showed them operating rooms, a store for medicines and cages where sick animals were kept during their stay. He explained that Jake was the vet on duty this morning.

"Can we see some pets being examined, Mr Hall?" asked Becky excitedly. She had really enjoyed being shown round the practice, but wanted to see more of the patients themselves.

"If you're quiet, we can sit in on Jake's surgery for a few minutes," agreed Mr Hall. He led them into a treatment room where Jake, a veterinary nurse and a small boy were bent over a table. A man who was probably the boy's dad, stood in the corner. Everyone crept in as quietly as possible.

As soon as the young vet caught their eye, his face broke into a wide grin.

"Come in, great to see you!" said Jake as he waved them over to the table. "Meet Harold the Iguana — the poor chap's a bit under the weather, isn't he, Sam?" The vet winked at the young lad that was peering over the table on tiptoe. A large green and yellow lizard sat motionless in front of him, its long tail draped over the boy's hand. Only the occasional movement of a beady eye gave a clue that the reptile was alive.

"You're at St Sebastian's aren't you?" asked Sophie. The boy nodded shyly and then let his gaze return to his pet.

"You'll have to say hello if you spot each other on Monday," smiled the nurse kindly. She was a young woman, with a thick mane of wavy red hair piled on top of her head. Becky realised she was trying to cheer Sam up.

"This is Alice Radcliffe, the best nurse in Sussex!" said Jake. "I think you and Mrs Fitz have already met haven't you?"

"Oh, yes. Will Harold be all right, Alice?" asked Mrs Fitzgerald.

Alice nodded. "He's suffering from a lack of vitamins, so Jake's going to inject him with a special mixture to boost up his system again." She turned to Sam's dad. "After that he should be back to his old self, but you must make sure he gets lots of calcium and green veg, Mr Lester."

"We definitely will," he answered, rubbing his son's shoulder reassuringly.

Suddenly, Jake had a wicked glint in his eye. "It's just occurred to me that Harold looks a bit like you, Donald!" he giggled.

Even Dan couldn't resist a titter, as Donald raised his eyes to heaven. "I think we'd better leave my rude young colleague to it," the old man muttered with a smile. "Anyway, it's time for the final attraction on my tour."

They were led out of a side door and up some stairs. Becky and Sophie felt a tingle of excitement.

"It's very comfortable up here, Donald," Dan remarked, bumping his head on a low beam. "Do you live above the practice?"

The tall man bent his head instinctively as he led them into a cosy, red sitting room. "No, but I've furnished upstairs so that any of us can stay overnight if an animal comes in needing constant attention," the vet explained. "I've also got my office up here." Mr Hall turned to Sophie and patted her shoulder. "Now, Sophie, I want you to meet Rosie." He led the girl to the fireplace, where a little tortoiseshell cat was curled up contentedly in a wicker basket.

"She's beautiful!" Sophie exclaimed. Rosie stretched her body up to meet the girl's hand, and began purring deeply. Sophie couldn't wait to tell Isabel.

"This little cat follows me everywhere — I've never had a pet like her."

"That's just how we feel about Albert," said Becky, with a smile.

"Now you can see why I'm reluctant to leave her while I'm away in Australia," Donald explained to Dan. "Particularly as the kittens are due in a few weeks."

"Mmm," sympathised Dan as he got down on all fours to stroke the small cat. "She's such an affectionate little thing."

As he got down to the tortoiseshell's level, Sophie caught his eye meaningfully.

"Dad, can't we help?" she whispered.

Dan sighed. "I'm not sure..."

Becky joined her sister. "Oh, please, Dad! We could look after Rosie while Mr Hall's away!" She turned to Mrs Fitzgerald, pleadingly.

"Now, hold on, it's not *my* decision, girls!" she cried, putting her hands up. "Anyway, it wouldn't just be while Donald's in Sydney. Rosie would have to come and stay for a good while before the birth, so that she has a settled base for when her kittens are born."

"That's right," agreed Donald. "Now, don't pester your father. It's too big a commitment, particularly with his busy job."

The girls would have continued, but they were interrupted by the entrance of Alice, who had rushed up the stairs.

"Donald, would you mind coming down please?" she panted. "Jake's still tied up treating the iguana and we've had a road traffic accident come in."

"Of course." Mr Hall was up instantly. "Excuse

me, please."

Becky and Sophie also jumped to their feet, full of concern. "Can we help?" asked Becky.

"Would you ask Mrs Williams to show you into Jake's surgery?" Mr Hall suggested. "I'd like someone to keep that little boy company, he could do with being distracted."

The two girls nodded eagerly and headed downstairs after Mr Hall and Alice.

"I hope that whoever's been rushed in is OK," said Dan, sitting in an armchair.

Mrs Fitzgerald nodded and sighed, and Dan lowered his voice. "Angela... Now we're on our own, what do you think I should do about looking after Rosie?"

Mrs Fitzgerald smiled knowingly as he went on. "I'd love to say yes to the girls, but I don't see how we can take that on with my job. I don't have any spare time as it is!"

"I know, Dan," she smiled. "And while I could happily take Rosie, I've got a much better idea than that."

"Eh?" Dan looked over, puzzled.

"I think I've found a way of housing Rosie and increasing your spare time no end," Mrs Fitzgerald declared. "Let me explain..."

7

Decision Time

Dan left his seat and began pacing furiously up and down the sitting room. "Angela, have you gone mad?" he demanded.

Mrs Fitzgerald quietly shook her head, then took a sip from her teacup. "Hear me out Dan, it's not as crazy as it sounds."

"But I can't just give up my job — I've got a responsibility to my girls!" Dan's footsteps were getting faster as he got more and more worked up. As he headed to the fireplace for the hundredth time, Rosie scuttled under the sofa for safety.

"Please sit down," begged Mrs Fitzgerald.

"You're frightening the cat."

Dan stopped pacing and sat heavily in his armchair.

"Now, you can't deny that travelling to London is wearing you out," she said. "You're looking shattered. The accountancy job is simply too much for you, now you live in Haresfield."

"But I don't want to move back to London," sighed Dan, running his hands through his black hair so it stood upright.

Mrs Fitzgerald nodded. "I know. And that's why I think it's best you resign immediately."

"What? And how exactly will I pay the bills after that?" groaned Dan, starting to look a bit impatient.

"I've come up with a new business idea for you that won't take you away from the girls at *all*," she answered proudly. Mrs Fitzgerald reached into her handbag. She always took her old tapestry carpet bag with her on trips out, which was crammed full of everything from clothes pegs to peppermints. Eventually she fished out a notepad and pencil.

"I suggest that you and I set up a holiday centre for pets together," she announced, swiftly holding her finger to her mouth to show Dan that he should listen. "I love my home, but Tangletrees is so enormous I can't keep it up properly. It's got a good couple of acres of meadowland, most of which I don't use. All my pets have been happy there and I think it would be wonderful to turn it into a place where other animals could come and stay too."

Dan was speechless.

"I realise that the centre won't make a fortune," continued Mrs Fitzgerald, "but if you came in as my business partner you'd have a simpler, healthier way of life. Imagine how happy Becky and Sophie would be — they love animals just as much as I do!" Although Mrs Fitzgerald was trying to stay calm, she couldn't stop the excitement creeping into her voice. "We could be up and running by Christmas!"

"But it took me years to train as an accountant.

I don't even know if I could do anything else," argued Dan.

Mrs Fitzgerald snorted. "Of course you can! With your accounting skills you could take over the business side of things easily," Angela persisted. "Now, I've been on the phone to a few kennels, the council and the RSPCA to find out what we'd need to do." She flicked through the pages in her notebook carefully. "We would have to pool some of our savings to pay for all the work needed — I've even got a few quotes from local builders."

"You're really serious aren't you?" said Dan. His mind was racing. Angela's plan sounded like a wonderful fairy tale, but he couldn't believe it could actually come true.

"Dan Ashford, when you get to know me properly you'll realise I only suggest ideas I believe in," she responded, firmly. "Anyway, it was the girls that gave me the inspiration. They're brilliant with pets, so when Donald came round the other day and mentioned Rosie, I knew they'd want to help. Thinking up the holiday centre idea was simply the next step."

"Well, I suppose Tangletrees would make an ideal location," mumbled Dan, weighing things up.

"Exactly. And I'm convinced people in the area would trust us with their pets. We could ask Haresfield surgery to work with us, so there'd be expert advice on hand if we had any problems." Mrs Fitzgerald leant over and picked up the tea tray Donald had prepared before he was called away. "Right! I'm going to make us another cup of tea and leave you in here to think it over."

The eccentric old lady marched past Dan into Donald's kitchen. As Dan sat deep in thought in the sitting room, he heard the whistle of the kettle and then Mrs Fitzgerald's voice. "Oh, and by the way, I've thought of the most excellent name for the place: *Pet Hotel.* Don't you think that's just perfect?"

Two hours later, as the girls bounced around the surgery, Dan could not believe what he had just said. Had he really just agreed to Mrs Fitzgerald's harebrained scheme?

Yet part of Dan couldn't deny the huge sense of relief he felt inside. He knew he would be far happier in Haresfield than he'd ever been in his dusty office in Aldgate. Anyway, if everything went wrong, he could always go for another accountancy job. And who knows? Maybe Tangletrees Pet Hotel really could work.

The girls had been absolutely amazed when he and Mrs Fitzgerald had come downstairs and revealed their plan. It had taken a few minutes for the news to sink in.

"So as well as taking care of Rosie, we'll be able to look after dogs and cats from all over?" asked Becky, excitedly.

"Not just dogs and cats — any creature can come to stay!" announced Mrs Fitzgerald in triumph.

"What, even Harold the Iguana?" laughed Jake. Knowing how much Mrs Fitzgerald cared for animals, he thought this Pet Hotel scheme was a great idea.

"Of course! Anything that leaps, runs, flies or swims! It's like the name suggests — a hotel just for animals!" she said, pleased with herself.

"Brilliant!" cried Sophie, hugging her dad.

Donald however, was silent. Mrs Fitzgerald

could see the gruff old vet was concerned. She turned to him quietly and asked for his support and blessing.

"Angela, you will always have my support in anything you do, but my blessing? Forget it!"

"Please, Donald," urged Dan. "I'm confident we can make this work."

"It's insanity! Think of your career, man!" retorted the old man. He was so put out he sat down in the corner of the treatment room and turned his face to the wall. "What makes it worse is that I'll be out in Australia in a few weeks. I won't be on hand to help."

"Yes, but Alice and I *will*," soothed Jake. "Come on, Donald, I know you're worried because you care, but can you think of a better qualified team?"

"Humpf!" Donald grunted something and then turned back to Mrs Fitzgerald and the Ashford clan. Everyone stood in nervous silence for a few moments, waiting for the old vet to respond.

"Well, I suppose you'll never know until you try," he sighed, then brightened. "And we could always do with an accountant here from time to time, and that'll keep you on the straight and narrow!"

When they got home that afternoon, Dan sat down to write his resignation letter. Now he had made the decision, he realised he would be counting the days until he could escape the piles of paperwork and over-crowded trains he had been battling against from Monday to Friday. The look on his daughters' faces had been enough to persuade him he'd done the right thing. Sophie was so over the moon she had ridden straight round to Isabel's to pass on the news.

In the lounge, the phone rang. Becky ran to answer it, Albert trailing behind her.

It was Sarah, the girls' mum. Becky tried to tell her the terrific news, tripping over the words in her excitement.

But instead of being pleased, Sarah sounded shocked and worried that Dan had given up his job just like that. "Put Dad on," she instructed.

"Is this really true, Dan?" Sarah asked.

"Yes, it is," Dan answered. "But I really believe it's going to be a change for the better." He crossed his fingers as he spoke, outlining their plans in great detail, but his ex-wife was naturally worried.

"I need to know that you can support the girls," she pleaded. "I can't just pop over from France to help out if something goes wrong!"

"Please, *trust* me, Sarah," Dan reasoned. "Just give me till Christmas, we'll be up and running by then. You'll be able to see for yourself that it was the right move."

There was a pause at the other end of the line. "OK, I'll hold judgement until then, Dan. But by Christmas, I'll need to know for sure that you can carry on looking after Becky and Sophie."

Dan said goodbye and hung up. Now he realised their dream of Pet Hotel *had* to come true...

8

A Houseful Of Pets

"Girls, can you come here, please!" hollered Mrs Fitzgerald from the kitchen at April Close. Up to her arms in pizza base mixture, she was right in the middle of preparing Saturday lunch. She squeezed her way round the large breakfast table in her green padded jacket with Dan's black and white chef's apron tied awkwardly over the top. From beneath her flowery frock gleamed a pair of bright red wellingtons.

"Girls!"

Becky and Sophie finally emerged from the garden.

"Can you cheer up Albert? Charlie's stolen his dog basket again," Mrs Fitzgerald sighed. "Every time I turf the little devil out, he slinks back into it."

On hearing his name, the retriever sat bolt upright in the wicker basket. Albert was beside him, using his sharp teeth to pull fiercely at his purple blanket and growling. But Charlie didn't seem to notice, and as he panted excitedly it even looked as though he was smiling.

"Poor Bertie. Come and play with us," laughed Sophie. "I've made him a much nicer new bed in the front room, but he won't have it." She held out her arms to the terrier, who gave up on his basket and took an impressive running jump towards her.

"I just think Charlie is finding it strange getting used to his temporary home," sympathised Becky. But, when she bent down to play with the retriever's ears, she had to admit he looked far from unhappy.

"Well, he'll be all right soon. But we all have to work hard on perfecting our animal skills," pointed out Mrs Fitzgerald. "Every pet that comes to stay will be feeling a bit lonely when they first arrive at Pet Hotel, won't they?" The building work at Tangletrees was now well underway, and Mrs Fitzgerald and her clan of pets had moved themselves to the Ashford house until it was done.

Working with the team at Haresfield surgery, Dan and Mrs Fitzgerald had carefully planned out the new pet centre. It would have large, airy enclosures for all sizes of animal, with long runs out behind the back of the building. Most of the meadow was going to stay the same, although there would soon be a new stable block in place. Jake and Donald's advice had been crucial, particularly on choosing dry places for storing food, bedding and for thinking of ways to make the place as animal-friendly as possible.

Sophie passed the little dog to Becky's lap,

where he soon calmed down and dropped off to sleep. "I think most animals seem to cheer up when you show them love," said her older sister.

"I've always thought the same thing," agreed Mrs Fitzgerald. "Look how well Rosie has got on with Sophie." Mr Hall had moved Rosie in a few days ago, and Sophie had gone out of her way to give the little cat lots of attention. The old vet was really pleased at how well she was settling in.

"I don't think Mr Hall will mind going to Australia now he knows I'm keeping an eye on her," Sophie said, her face flushing with pride.

BANG!

A thundering crash shook the room from outside, sending Albert up in the air in fright. He leapt into the basket that Charlie had now abandoned in favour of running around the kitchen and barking. The girls scrambled to the back door, as Dan tramped through — covered in grasscuttings and mud. Mrs Fitzgerald's two stout ginger toms scooted through the door behind him, almost knocking the girls' dad off balance.

"Blast!" he swore, trying to yank his boots off. Eventually his right welly gave way, sending him backwards onto his bottom with a muffled curse.

"What on earth was that noise?" asked Mrs Fitzgerald.

"The engine on the lawnmower's just blown up," Dan muttered.

"But, Dad! now Oscar's here, *he* can eat the lawn for you," smiled Sophie, running over to tug at his left boot.

"I'm afraid he'll eat all of the rose bushes as well," sighed Dan, finally managing to peel off his woolly hat and waxed jacket. He sat down at the kitchen table, sinking an elbow into one of Mrs Fitzgerald's pizza bases by mistake. "I don't think I'm cut out for this country life business."

"Rubbish!" snorted Mrs Fitzgerald. "Things will be much easier when you've left work and start to get into things here full-time." She gently tried to pull the dough out from underneath Dan's arm, but he looked so gloomy she decided to leave it where it was.

"Come on, Dad, you're doing a great job," soothed Becky. She was very sensitive and could understand exactly how difficult all this must be for him.

Dan had two weeks to go until he gave up his city job. In the meantime, he was only able to help at evenings and weekends. He divided his free time between overseeing the building work at Tangletrees and sorting out the business side of things. He'd also signed up for several pet care courses and was sitting in with Donald and Jake at Haresfield surgery whenever he got the chance. Becky squeezed her dad's hand. He was looking more tired than ever.

"Becky's right, of course," agreed Mrs Fitzgerald. "You've just got to relax."

"I know, I know," Dan mumbled. "I just feel that my stress levels seem to be going up instead of down!"

Sophie could see her dad was about to launch into a lengthy speech, but he was distracted by a gentle neighing sound. The back door was nudged open to reveal Billy poking his head into the room and whinnying in delight. Half the washing line was wrapped round his chestnut head and body.

"Now I've got a Shetland pony in my kitchen!" Dan cried in desperation.

Sophie smiled nervously. "And he's turned into a clothes horse!"

Becky's heart skipped a beat. "His rope must have come loose," she wailed. "Sorry, Dad! It won't happen again — ever."

"Just be careful, Becks," Dan warned. "Billy

could have hurt himself."

Becky ran outside to tie up the stray pony, and remove the now dirty laundry. Her eyes prickled with tears of shame at her carelessness. She didn't know what she'd have done if anything had happened to Billy, and also knew that this was the last thing her dad needed.

But when Becky came back into the kitchen the mood seemed to have lifted. Dad was passing round thick slices of pepperoni pizza and Sophie was reading out a letter that had arrived that morning from their mum.

"She's arriving on the 19th December!" crowed Sophie in delight.

Becky's spirits lifted immediately. "I can't wait for her to see Pet Hotel."

"Well, we should be in business by then," Dan replied.

"It'll be great to meet her," smiled Mrs Fitzgerald. As she turned to fetch a tuna and sweetcorn pizza from the oven, a flash of inspiration hit her. "I know, why don't we make the 19th our official open day? It would be perfect timing."

Sophie was thrilled. "Mum'll be so impressed!"

"Can we do leaflets and flags for it?" Becky asked.

"Of course," Mrs Fitzgerald answered. "It wouldn't be a proper open day otherwise."

Dan stayed very quiet at the table. He knew the centre had to be ready by then, but could they really do it?

"I reckon she's going to have at least three kittens," guessed Sophie, excitedly. It was the half-term holiday, and she and Becky were out playing on their bikes with Isabel. They'd propped them under the tree on Haresfield village green and were sitting together on the iron bench nearby.

"I wonder if they'll look anything like Barnaby," mused Becky.

"Definitely!" Isabel answered. "When they're born I'm going to ask my mum and dad if we can have one."

"Come on, then, let's cycle back home and see how Rosie's doing," decided Sophie, reaching for her bike so she'd have a headstart. "I'm sure Mrs Fitz will let you stay for lunch, Isabel."

"Great!" said her friend.

The three girls whizzed down the hill towards April Close.

As they parked their bikes against the sidewall of the house, Mrs Fitzgerald came bustling towards them. Although she was smiling, her face looked anxious.

"What's wrong?" asked Becky, nervously.

"Well, it's nothing to worry about," Mrs Fitzgerald answered slowly, "but Rosie seems to have disappeared."

Isabel and Sophie almost dropped their bikes in shock.

"Disappeared?" echoed Becky, in horror.

"Now, please don't get upset. Your dad and Donald are off looking for her now," the old lady tried to speak calmly. "It's actually quite normal for a mother-to-be to go and find somewhere quiet at this time, so she can have her babies in peace."

"But wasn't *I* looking after her well enough?" Sophie asked in a trembling voice.

"You did a fantastic job, Sophie," said Mrs Fitzgerald, smiling at her. "But, nature often has its own way of doing things. Now, come on, do try and lose those long faces, girls, *please*."

The three girls trooped sadly in with Mrs Fitzgerald. None of them could get the sweet little cat out of their minds.

9

Race Against Time

The girls had searched everywhere, but there was still no sign of Rosie. The little cat had been missing for three days. Mr Hall was due to fly to Sydney on Sunday, and was growing more and more tense and irritable.

To make things worse, the building work on Tangletrees had hit a setback. One of the builders, Mr Chase, had broken his leg playing rugby and was unable to work. With one man down, the conversion was falling behind schedule. And now the building company had called Dan to say that the last delivery of bricks had been delayed.

After an emergency meeting, Mrs Fitzgerald

and the Ashfords decided to visit Tangletrees to take a look round themselves.

"It's awful!" cried Sophie, as she picked her way through the rubble piled up at the back of the old house. In the cold, grey afternoon the building seemed almost derelict.

"It certainly doesn't look like my home any more," sighed Mrs Fitzgerald. She tucked her umbrella over her arm and pulled open the back door. Looking at the mess inside she added, "The trouble is, it doesn't look like a pet centre either."

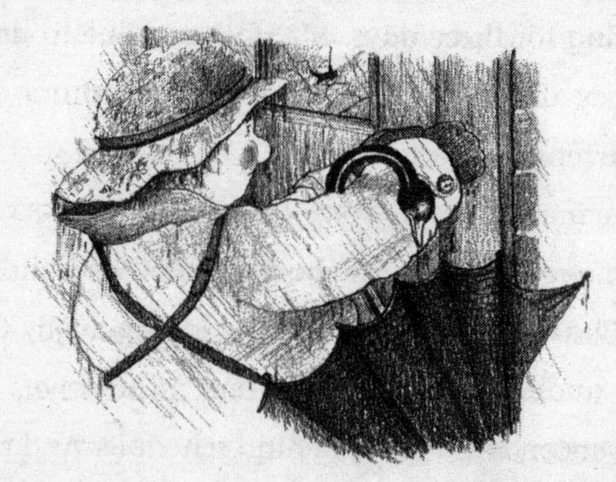

The rooms were littered with building materials, odd planks of wood and heaps of sand. None of the animal areas had been built, and even the heating and lights hadn't been put in yet. It was a far cry from the welcoming pet kennels they had all imagined.

"You'll be surprised at how much better this will look when the builders have cleared up behind them," said Dan, trying to sound cheerful, as he led the sad little group round the house with a torch. Inside, he felt just as miserable as the others, but knew he couldn't let it show.

Becky and Sophie followed after their dad into the hall of Tangletrees. This space was going to become the reception of Pet Hotel, but it was a disaster area at the moment. Everything was covered in a thick layer of plaster, and sacks of cement lined the walls. Becky opened the front door to let some of the dust escape.

"The hall isn't too bad," Dan continued. "You should have seen it a week ago." The others just glared at him.

"Oh dear," sighed Mrs Fitzgerald, shivering underneath her rain mac. "Maybe I was a bit hasty in suggesting an open day before Christmas."

"We can't cancel it now," said Sophie, breaking down into tears. She and her sister had spent days handing out leaflets at school and around Haresfield. They'd even got their friends to cycle over to the nearby town, Clayton, to spread the word. So many people had promised to come, it would be terrible to let them all down at the last minute. And with their mum coming, too...

Becky slumped down on the front doorstep, with Albert on her lap. "I knew it was all too good to be true," she mumbled, just loud enough for the others to hear.

It was this comment that finally made up Dan's mind.

"Come on, Angela, we're not going to give up now!" he announced, greeting their disappointed faces with a brave smile.

"I don't want to, Dan," explained Mrs Fitzgerald. "But we do have to be realistic."

"Listen, I'll hire a van for a day and go and collect the bricks myself," he argued, striding around the hall as he got more excited. "After I've finished at the office next week I'll be able to spend every hour of the day here, until the place is completely ready."

Sophie wiped her eyes and tried to smile, but Mrs Fitzgerald still looked unsure.

"But will it be enough, Dan?" she said. "What, with Mr Chase being away and Tangletrees being in such a state... And now that Rosie's disappeared, it seems as though everything's against us."

Becky was so fed up she stopped listening. She felt as if all the hopes she had built up over the last few weeks were tumbling down around her. As she stroked Albert, her eyes roamed the messy garden — if only they had another three months! The open day was in just eight weeks time. And before that they had to get through an inspection by the local council to get the special licence they needed to open a pet kennels.

As she was thinking, Becky's eyes settled on a basket tucked in the corner by Tangletrees' grand front door. It appeared to be a fairly ordinary picnic hamper, except that it was wobbling about mysteriously.

"Quick, Dad, come and have a look at this!" she shouted as she leapt up to investigate. When she carefully pulled back the wicker lid, Becky couldn't believe her eyes. Inside, wrapped in a tartan blanket, were lots of chocolate-coloured guinea pigs.

"Good grief!" cried Dan in surprise.

"Someone obviously thought we were open for business already. They've left them here for us to look after," said Mrs Fitzgerald, tutting in annoyance. "Some people just aren't fit to keep pets. These little poppets could have died."

Becky and Sophie took turns to peep in at the sleepy little creatures. "I think I counted six, Mrs Fitz," said Becky.

"Do you think they're going to be all right, Angela?" Dan asked in concern.

"I think so, but we'd better run them up to the

surgery for Jake to give them the once over." Mrs Fitzgerald buttoned her enormous coat and led the way to the Land Rover. Becky walked slowly behind, clutching the basket protectively.

"When I see abandoned creatures like that, girls, it makes me determined to get Pet Hotel up and running as soon as possible."

"I'm glad that this has brought back your fighting talk, Angela," Dan smiled. But his smile quickly faded as her words sunk in. "But don't forget that Pet Hotel is going to be a kennels for *paying* guests," he reminded his partner, seriously. "We won't be able to take in every waif and stray that turns up at the front door." Dan could see any profit from the centre being eaten up by abandoned animals.

"Nonsense!" Mrs Fitzgerald decided. "How could we possibly turn away these little beauties?"

Dan shrugged, knowing Mr Hall would despair when he heard that the place was going to become not just a kennels, but a rescue centre too! Even so, he was glad that the guinea pigs had stirred Mrs Fitzgerald's enthusiasm. Dan was sure that with a massive push from everyone they could get the place ready.

The Ashfords piled into the Land Rover, and Mrs Fitzgerald lent forward to turn the ignition key.

"Hold it!"

Everyone turned to look at Sophie.

"We've forgotten Albert," she explained, hopping out.

Becky placed the basket on the back seat and tumbled out of the car. "I hope he's not in trouble again," she whispered in her sister's ear.

Sophie nodded, but it wasn't hard to find Albert. Following the sound of his short barks, the girls were led to Billy's old stable at the end of the back garden.

Becky edged open the door. "Sophie... *look*!"

There, nestling in a corner, lay Rosie — with four tiny kittens curled up in the sawdust in front of her! Each was a beautiful mixture of Rosie and Barnaby's colourings — two tortoiseshell, one tabby and a little black one.

Albert sat by Rosie's side, wagging his tail proudly, as if he knew he had been a good boy. For a few seconds, Sophie and Becky were both silent, taking in the sight of the new cat family.

"Well, well," said Dan as he came in behind the girls and knelt down. "This was where you decided to go, Rosie. Donald will be *so* pleased!"

"So will Isabel!" grinned Sophie.

"You'd better go and tell Mrs Fitz the news," Dan grinned, checking the kittens to see if they looked healthy. Everything seemed to be OK, although the litter was so young that the kittens' eyes weren't even open yet.

As Sophie hared off, Becky turned to her dad. "This must be a good sign for Pet Hotel, mustn't it Dad?" she asked, hope burning in her dark eyes.

"If two animal families have found their way here already, there must be something going for the old place," Dan agreed.

"Now it's up to us to get it ready in time," said Becky.

10

Pet Hotel

Three loud knocks rang out from Tangletrees' old front door.

"That'll be him," Sophie gasped, tugging at her sister's sleeve. Overcome with nerves and excitement, she didn't realise that she'd practically yelled the words at Becky.

"Sssshhhh!" warned Becky, putting her finger to her mouth. "We don't want to spoil things, Soph." It was the day of the local government visit, to decide whether Pet Hotel was fit to become a proper pet kennels. The girls had dashed back from St Sebastian's to be there, although their dad had told them that the inspector wasn't due until half past four.

Shortly before he was due to arrive, Becky and Sophie had been told to stay in the upstairs part of the house. All of the top floor of Tangletrees had been converted into a special flat for Mrs Fitzgerald. When Pet Hotel was up and running, she would live here — she'd be on hand to tend the animals twenty-four hours a day.

Downstairs, the girls could hear muffled hellos.

"Can't we creep along the landing and take a look through the banisters?" Sophie asked. "I can't just sit and do nothing, it's driving me mad!"

Becky shook her head vigorously, but as usual her little sister had made up her own mind. She crawled on her stomach out of Mrs Fitzgerald's new sitting room and out along the landing, then poked her head out between the banisters.

Becky edged up alongside her, glaring at her to show how cross she was.

They could see their dad in the hall below, shaking hands with the inspector, Mr Jenkinson, who was a grey-haired man with glasses. He was carrying a clipboard and already peering into every corner of the room, firing a string of difficult questions at their dad and Mrs Fitzgerald as he did so. His face seemed creased in a permanent frown. Suddenly, the girls had to duck their heads through the banisters, as he stared straight up at them.

"He'd better not have seen us," muttered Becky.

Mrs Fitzgerald was dressed in her Sunday best, pearl necklace and all. But Sophie and Becky both had to stifle a giggle when they suddenly realised that she was still wearing her yellow souwester hat where she'd been busy outside adding the finishing touches to the place.

After talking for a while, the sisters saw their dad lead Mr Jenkinson out of the reception area towards the animal block, where all the pens were ready for him to take a look at.

"Come on, there's nothing more for us to see," decided Becky, tugging on her sister's school jumper. "Let's go and watch telly while we wait for the decision."

"It might take our minds off it, I suppose," sighed Sophie.

As they sat idly flicking the channels on the television, time seemed to drag by. Five o'clock came and went, but still there was no sound from downstairs.

"Oh, this is just unfair!" sulked Sophie as she took another look out of the window to see whether Mr Jenkinson's car had gone.

"You should just be grateful that we got the place ready in time," Becky reminded her.

The last few weeks had been the busiest of the girls' lives. After realising he couldn't cope by himself, Dan had hired extra builders and worked all hours in order to finish Tangletrees. Mrs Fitzgerald had been frantic too, organising the team of plumbers, electricians and carpenters needed to make the building a comfortable and safe place for animals. Even Jake had helped out in his spare time, although he and Alice had their hands full running Haresfield surgery now Mr Hall had left for Australia.

Sophie and Becky had taken charge of the pets at April Close. With the arrival of the abandoned guinea pigs and Rosie's new family, the girls really had their work cut out. Sophie, with help from Isabel, took special care of the kittens while Becky dashed round with Bertie, tending to all the others. Even Sam Lester, the boy they'd met on their first visit to the vets, had lent a hand.

With a lot of effort from everyone, they'd managed to transform Mrs Fitzgerald's home into Pet Hotel, exactly as they'd planned back in October. Work had finally finished yesterday, and all the pets had been moved over to their new home. Albert, of course, would be staying at April Close with the Ashfords.

"It's half-past five!" moaned Becky. "How can it take this long?"

"I'm going crazy! Can't we go out on the landing again?" pleaded Sophie.

"No way!" replied Becky. "I'll drag you back in if you try."

Luckily, she didn't have to — just then, Mrs

Fitzgerald burst into the sitting room. She looked tense and flushed.

The girls looked up expectantly.

"Well?" they both said at once.

Mrs Fitzgerald just shrugged her shoulders and turned to Dan. He'd poked his head round the door behind her, clutching a piece of paper.

"We haven't got it have we?" cried Sophie, kicking the sofa in despair. "That man looked so mean, he was never going to give us permission. I knew it!"

Dan and Mrs Fitzgerald nodded seriously.

But something didn't seem right to Becky. "What's that in your hand, Dad?" she asked.

"What, this?" replied Dan, looking down at his hand in mock surprise.

"Yes *that*!"

"Oh, that's nothing. It's just our certificate of authorisation, that's all." Her dad began to giggle, and Mrs Fitzgerald grinned from ear to ear.

Becky and Sophie could hardly believe it. They'd done it! They'd passed the inspection!

"Congratulations!" Dan cried, waving the piece of paper. "We are now the official owners of a pet kennels!"

"Looks like we'd better get ready for the 19th," announced Mrs Fitzgerald, laughing and crying as the girls whooped round the room in delight.

"Excellent!" screamed Sophie. "I knew we could do it!"

As everyone hugged each other, Becky still couldn't believe the good news. Now there was only one thing left for them to do — organise the best open day Haresfield had ever seen!

"Roll up, roll up!" Jake's voice rang out around the front garden of Tangletrees. The young vet was standing at a table in his crisp, white coat, "Free pet advice from a qualified expert!"

The Pet Hotel Open Day had finally arrived, and the entire place was covered in Christmas decorations and streamers. It seemed as though the whole village had turned up, and all kinds of people had volunteered to take part in the day.

Alice Radcliffe had set up a home-made bread and soup stand in the Pet Hotel reception area, and was busily handing round delicious mugfuls of broth to passing visitors.

Mrs Fitzgerald and Dan were offering guided tours of the place and signing up their first pet guests. By midday, they had already taken a booking for two Alsatians, several cats and a family of gerbils. They'd even had some luck in finding decent homes for the guinea pigs and Rosie's kittens. The first kitten, however, had been promised to Isabel Wilde. She was at the Open Day with her mum and dad, and had finally chosen the little black one. It was a boy, and she had decided to call him Shadow.

"Only ten pence a go, ladies and gentlemen," shouted Sophie to passing visitors, "for the chance to win one of Mrs Fitzgerald's enormous fruitcakes!"

She and Becky had set up a competition to guess the weight of Billy. The lively little pony stood next to them in the garden, whinnying happily.

"I think Billy's enjoying this," grinned Becky, scratching the chestnut pony's ears.

Sophie turned away to take down another competition entry and then leant towards her sister. "And nobody's even guessed close to his weight, yet!" She felt a tug at her ankle and saw Albert desperately pulling at her leggings. "Look who's feeling left out — our number one pet!"

"Poor old Bertie," Becky sympathised. "Are you lonely down there?" She bent down to pick him up, but the little white dog jumped out of her hands and shot off.

"That's not like him," Sophie frowned, leaving her entry book to follow the terrier.

Albert belted up the path and landed at the feet of a tall, blonde lady in a raincoat. Despite her neat, black trousers she immediately fell to her knees and bundled the Westie on to her lap. Albert was going mad with excitement, licking her face and wagging his tail.

It was at that moment that each sister realised.

"MUM!"

Sophie was there in a flash, tumbling into her mother's arms.

"Hello, my darling," cried Sarah Ashford, pushing back her dark glasses to give her youngest daughter a kiss. "You look so well — and so *big*!"

Becky passed Billy's reins over to Jake and ran over to join them, throwing her arms round her mum's neck.

"We've really missed you, Mum," Becky murmured softly. She couldn't say any more because the tears were welling up inside her.

The three of them stayed locked in a hug for ages and ages. Eventually, they saw Dan and Mrs Fitzgerald making their way towards them.

After all the hellos and introductions, Dan decided it was time for Sarah to have a tour of the establishment.

"I think that Becky and Sophie should take you round," he announced, looking fondly at the two girls. "Without their help and support, there wouldn't *be* a Pet Hotel."

"He's right you know," chuckled Mrs Fitzgerald, in her mauve hat and tulip-print suit.

Sarah smiled, and took her daughters' hands. "I can't wait to see it all," she said. "By the looks of it, you've done a fantastic job."

"Come on, Mum, we want to show you absolutely everything!" Sophie said, pulling Sarah's hand.

"OK, OK," she laughed. "You know, until now, I never thought I'd see it — a real hotel for pets!"

"The best thing, Mum," said Becky, smiling proudly as they walked through the happy throng of people, "is that Pet Hotel has only just started!"

PET HOTEL

Animal Casebook

If you're an animal lover, the thought of running a real pet hotel sounds brilliant, but it's actually a very demanding job. You have to make the visiting pets feel as comfortable and as happy as you can during their stay — and that means twenty-four hours a day! Good kennel-keepers always remember that every pet belongs to someone. Owners will expect you to make sure their animals are exercised, well-fed, safe and healthy while they're away.

How to Find a Good Pet Kennels

If you're going away and have to trust someone with your pet, these hints should help you find a good animal centre:

FIRST...

- Ask your vet.
- Look in the Yellow Pages.
  Kennels and catteries often advertise in local directories.

THEN, check that...

- The centre is clean and tidy, with animals that seem happy and well cared for.
- The owners ask for your pet to be vaccinated against common dog and cat diseases.
- There's a vet on call.
- The kennel staff seem cheerful and friendly.
- The centre seems busy. If it's popular, that's likely to be because it's well-managed.

Never be afraid to ask questions or take a good look round. Your pet is very important and so are you!

A Day In The Life Of A Pet Hotel

This imaginary diary will help you to build up a picture of a normal day in an animal holiday centre.

7.00am Up for the early morning check. Is everybody happy? The cats are still snoozing, but the dogs have already started barking for breakfast. What a racket!

8.00am The first new arrivals of the day are here. Scruff the collie is staying for a fortnight while his family are on holiday in Spain. Cleo the Persian cat needs to be looked after while her owner is in hospital recovering from an operation.

9.00am The staff start the daily routine of cleaning out each kennel and cat pen. Dogs stay in the exercise area while their kennels are being cleaned. Aren't some Westies messy? Hamish has been a bit of a hooligan and chewed his basket again last night. His kennel looks like a bomb site!

The day's first emergency: Sheba the German Shepherd has caught one of her toenails and now it's broken and bleeding. We'll bandage it for now, but if it keeps bleeding, Sheba will need to see the vet.

10.00am Preparing the pets' first meal of the day is going well. Most of them eat the usual mix of tinned food and biscuits — but there are always fussy ones like Tyke the tiny Yorkshire terrier who will only eat cat food!

A few of the cats are quite old, and need special diets to help their kidneys to keep working properly. The kittens we're looking after will eat anything! They think mealtimes are just another game.

11.00am A bit of grooming for Florence the sheepdog is in order. Florence is going home today, so we want her to look extra smart when her owner comes to pick her up. A quick bath, a lot of backcombing and a quick blow dry — Florence loves the attention!

12.00pm Time to clean out the guinea pigs and the hamsters. One of the guinea-pigs is due to be a mum any day now, so she needs extra care. The rabbits all get a special lunch-time treat of a carrot each.

1.00pm Time for our own lunch, but Sheba's nail is still bleeding badly. We call Mr Brown, the vet. He says he'll be here this afternoon to check on her.

2.00pm Florence's owner arrives to pick her up. The telephone hasn't stopped ringing all day with more bookings, and our latest arrival, Newton, the Great Dane, is the biggest animal guest we've had here for ages. I hope we can find a kennel big enough for him!

3.00pm All the dogs are given long walks and then returned to their kennels. It's hard work cleaning up after them, but hose pipes and disinfectant do the trick!

4.00pm Mr Brown, the vet, arrives to look at Sheba. He gently removes her damaged nail, stops the bleeding and re-bandages her foot for her. Now she's a lot more comfortable, and she'll soon get better. The vet gives her an injection to stop any infections, but she'll also have to take tablets twice a day with her food for a few days. Mr Brown says her nail will grow again in no time — thank goodness!

5.00pm Time to serve the second daily meal to the pets that need it. It seems that some dogs would never stop eating if you let them — no wonder Floss the Labrador is more of a Flabrador these days!

6.00pm The centre is now closed to the public for the day. A few last minute phone calls and then we're ready to settle down for the night. And would you believe it? Daphne the guinea pig has just given birth to two lovely babies. Her proud owner will be delighted when she gets back.

We'll keep a good eye on the pets during the night too. Looking after animals is a full-time job, so we all take it in turns to be around if our animal guests need us!

Ten Terrific Pet Hotel Facts

1. Kennels and cat pens have to be cleaned out thoroughly. Dogs and cats can be messy 'guests'. Lots of disinfectant makes sure all the animals stay healthy.

2. Dogs need plenty of exercise. Decent kennels have roomy pens where Airedales and Chihuahuas can stretch their legs before breakfast!

3. Extra care is needed if dogs are taken for a walk. If they're not kept on a strong lead they might try to find their own way home!

4. Cats aren't fitness freaks. Most are quite happy to laze around in their pens all day.

5. When lots of animals are booked into the Pet Hotel there'll always be a lot of washing up. Food and water bowls have to be kept spotless!

6. Some pets might be under treatment from the vet. They're usually given their tablets at mealtimes. This can be quite tricky because not everybody likes taking their medication, especially cats, rabbits and guinea pigs.

7. All guests at the Pet Hotel have to be vaccinated before they book in for their holiday, to prevent disease.

8. Most kennels recommend that guests arrive with their favourite toys or blankets to remind them of home during their stay.

9. Dogs and cats often pick up illnesses when they mix with other pets, so a good animal centre makes sure their pens are far enough apart to stop this happening.

10. Answering the telephone and booking guests in and out can take up a lot of time because owners need to feel their pets are going to be well-treated while they're away from home. Kennel-owners will have a number of questions to ask, to ensure the animals receive the right kind of care.

Have you read all the

PET HOTEL

books?

2

Twice the Trouble

Sophie and Becky have their hands full with a pair of boisterous Cocker spaniels — Whisky and Ginger cause chaos from the moment they arrive.

But things get worse when a beautiful Siamese checks in. It's up to the girls to make sure that the cat has a quiet, restful stay. Problem is, with Whisky and Ginger around, keeping the peace at Pet Hotel is going to be twice as hard as normal!

3

The Non-Stop Runaway

A Norfolk terrier is checked in and everyone takes an instant shine to her. But Sophie and Becky are warned that Pickle isn't the dream guest she appears to be.

The new arrival's got the wander-bug — she simply can't resist running away. The wayward dog's escape acts are now so famous no other kennels will even take her on. But the problems only start for Pet Hotel when it's time for the terrier to go home!

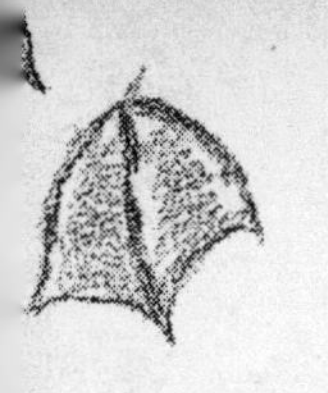

4

Pet Hotel Detectives

Sophie and Becky are delighted when their first exotic pet comes to the stay at the Hotel — Myriad, a beautiful Blue and Gold macaw.

Yet the visit turns sour when a sleepover at Tangletrees is interrupted by a midnight break-in! In horror, the team discover that the macaw's cage has been smashed, the bird nowhere to be seen. Can the sisters track down the thieves before it's too late for Myriad?

More animal-packed Pet Hotel books available from BBC Worldwide Ltd

The prices shown below were correct at the time of going to press. However BBC Worldwide Ltd reserve the right to show new retail prices on covers which may differ from those previously advertised in the text or elsewhere.

1 **Welcome to Pet Hotel** — Mandy Archer
0 563 38094 2 — £2.99

2 **Twice the Trouble** — Sara Carroll
0 563 38095 0 — £2.99

3 **The Non-Stop Runaway** — Emma Fischel
0 563 40550 3 — £2.99

4 **Pet Hotel Detectives** — Jessie Holbrow
0 563 40551 1 — £2.99

All BBC titles are available by post from:

Book Service By Post,
PO Box 29, Douglas, Isle of Man, IM99 1BQ

Credit cards accepted.
Please telephone 01624 675137 or fax 01624 670923.
Internet http://www.bookpost.co.uk
or e-mail: bookshop@enterprise.net for details.

Free postage and packaging in the UK.
Overseas customers: allow £1 per book (paperback) and £3 per book (hardback).